The BIG STORM

To Tom and Cristina and Our Big Beautiful Days!

SIMON & SCHUSTER BOOKS FOR YOUNG READERS
An imprint of Simon & Schuster Children's Publishing Division
1230 Avenue of the Americas, New York, New York 10020
Copyright © 2009 by Nancy Tafuri
SIMON & SCHUSTER BOOKS FOR YOUNG READERS is a trademark
of Simon & Schuster, Inc.
Book design by Chloë Foglia
The text for this book is set in Stonehouse.
The illustrations for this book are rendered in concentrated watercolor inks, pigma
micron pens, and Albrecht Dürer watercolor pencils.
Manufactured in China
10 9 8 7 6 5 4 3 2
Library of Congress Cataloging-in-Publication Data
Tafuri, Nancy.
The big storm: A very soggy counting book / Nancy Tafuri.—1st ed.
p. cm.
Summary: Ten animals find shelter in a hill hollow one by one, but when the storm is over,
a rumbling tells them there is still danger afoot.
ISBN: 978-1-4169-6795-8 (hardcover)
[1. Forest animals—Fiction. 2. Animals—Fiction. 3. Storms—Fiction. 4. Counting.]
I. Title.
PZ7.T117Ver 2009
[E]—dc22
2007047989

The BIG STORM

A Very Soggy COUNTING BOOK

Nancy Tafuri

Simon & Schuster Books for Young Readers

New York   London   Toronto   Sydney

The sky started to turn gray.
Dark black clouds started to gather.

Bird flew for cover.

Now there was **1** in the hill hollow.

The wind started to blow.

Mouse ran for cover.

Now there were **2** in the hill hollow.

Leaves started to swirl.

Squirrel ran for cover.

Then there were **3** in the hill hollow.

Lightning started to crack.

Rabbit ran for cover.

Then there were **4** in the hill hollow.

Rain started to fall.

Chipmunk ran for cover.

And this made **5** in the hill hollow until—

Thunder started to rumble and grumble—
Woodchuck, Raccoon, Opossum,
and Red Fox all ran for cover.

Now there were **6, 7, 8, 9** in the hill hollow, and then—

Skunk squeezed in and made it **10!**

10 critters huddled together,

tight and snug while

the clouds gathered.

The wind blew.

The leaves swirled.

The lightning cracked.

The rain fell and

the thunder rumbled

and grumbled . . .

all night long.

At last it was morning and
the sky was clear.
But all **10** could still hear

a RUMBLE
and a
GRUMBLE
in the air!

So they turned and found the sound was coming from . . .

2 BEARS!

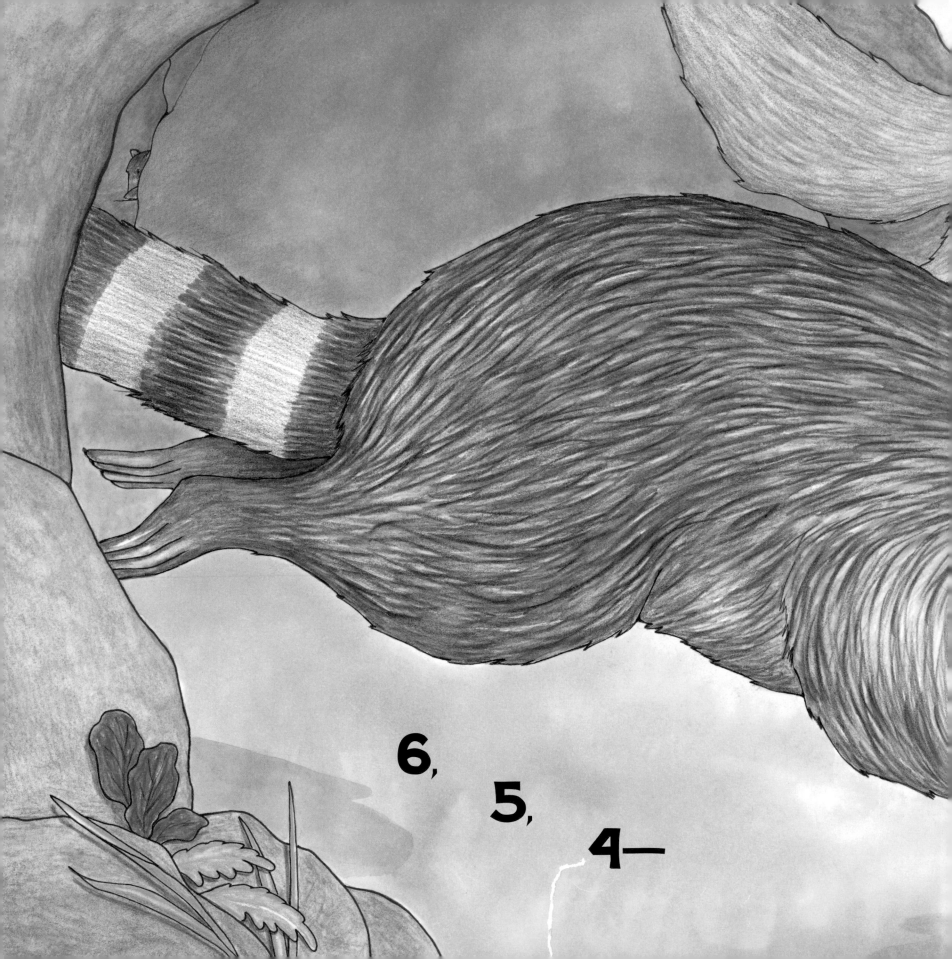

3,

2,

1—

away they all went.
And what did they find?

The **Big Storm**

had turned into . . .

A VERY BIG,
BEAUTIFUL
DAY!